THE GUARDIANS

TOOTHIANA

 part one

A Tooth Is Lost

Atheneum Books for Young Readers • An imprint of Simon & Schuster Children's Publishing Division • 1230 Avenue of the Americas, New York, New York 10020 • This book is a work of fiction. Any references to historical events, real people, or real places are used fictitiously. Other names, characters, places, and events are products of the author's imagination, and any resemblance to actual events or places or persons, living or dead, is entirely coincidental. • Copyright © 2012 by William Joyce • Rise of the Guardians TM & © 2012 DreamWorks Animation, LLC. "Pitch" character design and related elements used with permission. All rights reserved. • All rights reserved, including the right of reproduction in whole or in part in any form. • ATHENEUM BOOKS FOR YOUNG READERS is a registered trademark of Simon & Schuster, Inc. • Atheneum logo is a trademark of Simon & Schuster, Inc. • For information about special discounts for bulk purchases, please contact Simon & Schuster Special Sales at 1-866-506-1949 or business@simonandschuster.com. • The Simon & Schuster Speakers Bureau can bring authors to your live event. For more information or to book an event, contact the Simon & Schuster Speakers Bureau at 1-866-248-3049 or visit our website at www.simonspeakers.com. • Book design by Lauren Rille • The text for this book is set in Adobe Jenson Pro. • The illustrations for this book are rendered in a combination of charcoal, graphite, and digital media. • Manufactured in the United States of America 1012 OFF • 10 9 8 7 6 5 4 3 2 1 • CIP data for this book is available from the Library of Congress. • ISBN 978-1-4424-7291-4

THE GUARDIANS

TOOTHIANA

part one

A Tooth Is Lost

WILLIAM JOYCE

Atheneum Books for Young Readers
NEW YORK • LONDON • TORONTO • SYDNEY • NEW DELHI

The Changes That Come
with Peace

WILLIAM THE ABSOLUTE YOUNGEST galloped through the enchanted village of Santoff Claussen on the back of a large Warrior Egg, a gift from E. Aster Bunnymund. "I can't stop or I'll be scrambled!" he shouted over his shoulder to his friend Fog. In this new game of Warrior Egg tag, to be scrambled meant you had been caught by the opposing egg team and therefore, had lost a point.

Sascha and her brother, Petter, were in hot pursuit, riding Warrior Eggs of their own. The matchstick-thin legs of the mechanical eggs moved so fast, they were a blur.

"Comin' in for the scramble shot!" Petter warned. His long tag pole, with the egg-shaped tip, was inches away from Sascha.

"Eat my yolk," Sascha said with a triumphant laugh. She pushed a button, and suddenly, her Warrior Egg sprouted wings. She flew over the others, reaching the finish line first.

William the Absolute Youngest slowed to a trot. "Wings!" he grumbled. "They aren't even in the rules!"

"I invented them yesterday," said Sascha. "There's nothing in the rules that says you can't use 'em."

Soon Sascha was helping the youngest William construct his own set of eggbot wings. She liked the youngest William. He always tried to act older, and she appreciated his determination and spirit. Petter and Fog, feeling wild and industrious, catapulted themselves to the hollow of a tall tree where they had erected a hideout devoted to solving ancient mysteries, such as: why was there such a thing as bedtime, and what could they do to eliminate it forever?

Across the clearing, in a tree house perched high in the branches of Big Root—the tree at the center of the village—their friend Katherine contently watched the children play.

The air shimmered with their happy laughter. Many months had passed since the battle at the Earth's core during which Pitch, the Nightmare King, had been soundly defeated by Katherine and the other Guardians: Ombric, the wizard; his apprentice, Nicholas St. North; their friend Nightlight; and their newest ally, the Pookan rabbit known as E. Aster Bunnymund. Pitch, who had hungered for the dreams of innocent children and longed to replace them with nightmares, had vowed with his Fearlings to make all the children of Earth live in terror. But since the great battle, he had not been seen or heard from, and Katherine was beginning to hope that Pitch had been vanquished forever.

As for Katherine and her battle mates, their lives were forever changed. The Man in the Moon himself had given them the title of "Guardians." They were heroes now, sworn to protect the children of not just Santoff Claussen, but the entire planet. They had defeated Pitch, and their greatest challenge at present was how to manage the peace. The "nightmare" of Pitch's reign seemed to be over.

The other children of the village now filled their days with mischief and magic. Bunnymund, who could burrow through the Earth with astonishing speed, had created a series of tunnels for them, connecting the village with his home on Easter Island and with other amazing outposts around the world, and the children had become intrepid explorers. On any given day they might journey to the African savanna to visit the lions, cheetahs, and hippopotami—Ombric had taught them a number of animal languages, so they had numerous stories to hear and tell. Many of the creatures had already heard of their amazing adventures.

The children also regularly circled through Easter Island for the latest chocolate confection Bunnymund had invented, and could still be back in time for dinner and games with Bunnymund's mechanical egg comrades. The eggs were once Bunnymund's warriors; now they helped the children build all manner of interesting contraptions, from intricate egg-shaped puzzles where every piece was egg-shaped (a nearly impossible and frankly unexplainable feat) to egg-shaped submarines. But no matter where the children roamed or what they did to occupy their days, whenever they returned home to Santoff Claussen, it had never seemed so lovely to them.

As Katherine sat in her tree house, she put her arm around Kailash, her great Himalayan Snow Goose, and looked out on her beloved village. The forest that surrounded and protected Santoff Claussen had bloomed into a kind of eternal spring. The massive oaks and vines that had once formed an impenetrable wall against the outside world were thick with leaves of the deepest green. The huge, spear-size thorns that had once covered the vines grew pliant and blossomed with sweet-scented flowers.

Katherine loved the smell, and drew a deep breath of it. In the distance she could see Nicholas St. North walking with the beautiful, ephemeral Spirit of the Forest. She was more radiant now than ever before. Her gossamer robes were resplendent with blooms that shimmered like jewels. North was deep in conversation with her, so Katherine decided to investigate. She climbed on to Kailash's back and flew down into the clearing, just in time to see William the

Absolute Youngest try out the new wings with which he'd outfitted his Warrior Egg. He landed and trotted over to her.

"Want to race with us, Katherine?" he asked. He gave Kailash a scratch on her neck, and the goose honked a hello.

"I will later!" Katherine said, smiling. She waved to her friends and headed into the forest, realizing that it had been quite some time since any of the children had asked her to play, and an even longer time since she had accepted. In joining the world of the Guardians, she was in a strange new phase of her life—where she was neither child nor adult. As she watched the youngest William fly away with Sascha close behind him, she couldn't help but feel a bit torn.

Then she heard North's hearty laugh and, underneath that, the more musical tones of the Spirit of the Forest. Katherine hurried toward them, thinking that it was hard to believe that when North first came to Santoff Claussen with his band of outlaws, it had been with the intent to steal its treasures. The Spirit of the Forest, the village's last line of defense, had turned North's crew of cutthroats and bandits into stone statues—hideous, hunched elves. But she had spared North, for he alone among them was pure of heart.

When Katherine caught up with the Spirit and North, they were standing in that most strange and eerie part of the forest—the place where North's men stood frozen in time, like stones in a forgotten burial site. With the Spirit's help, North was bringing his bandits back to human form.

As the Spirit touched the head of each statue, North repeated the same spell, "From flesh to stone and back again. To serve with honor, your one true friend." And one by one they emerged from their frozen poses. To North's great amusement, they hadn't regained their size. They were still the same height as their stone selves—about two feet tall, with bulbous noses and high, childlike voices.

"Welcome back," North called out, slapping each of the elfin men on the back.

The men stamped their little feet and waved their little arms to get their blood flowing again, and soon the children, drawn by North's laughter, arrived. They were shocked; they often played among these small stone men, and now that they were moving—were alive, in fact—the children were most intrigued. Tall William, the first son of Old William, towered over them. Even the youngest William was overjoyed—at last he was taller than someone else.

While the children watched, the little men kneeled before North. They took on new names as they pledged to follow their former outlaw leader in a new life of goodness. Gregor of the Mighty Stink became Gregor of the Mighty Smile. Sergei the Terrible was now Sergei the Giggler, and so on.

It was an odd but auspicious moment, especially for North. He remembered his wild, unruly life as a bandit and the many dark deeds that he and these fellows had committed. He'd become a hero, a man of great learning, good humor, and some wisdom. So much had changed since that moment when he faced the temptation of the Spirit of the Forest, when he had rejected her promises of treasure and had chosen to save the children of Santoff Claussen.

North turned and looked at young Katherine. He felt the full weight of all they had been through. They had both changed. It was a change he did not fully understand, but he knew he was glad for it. For though these dwarfish fellows in front of him had once been his comrades in crime, North, in his heart, had been alone. But that was past. This was a different day. And through the friendship he now knew, he could change bad men to good and stone back to flesh.

North gently asked his old confederates to rise. They did so gladly.

Peace had indeed come.

Katherine took North's hand, and together they welcomed these baffled little men to the world of Santoff Claussen.

The Guardians Gather

ALTHOUGH THE CHILDREN HAD begun to refer to the battle at the Earth's core as "Pitch's Last Battle," the Guardians knew that the Nightmare King was both devious and shrewd. He could still be lurking somewhere, ready to pounce.

Nightlight, the mysterious, otherworldly boy who was Katherine's dearest friend, scoured the night sky for signs of Pitch's army. He even traveled deep into the cave where he'd been imprisoned in Pitch's icy heart for centuries, but all he found were memories of those dark times. Of Pitch and his Fearling soldiers, he could find not even an echo. Bunnymund kept his rabbit ears tuned for ominous signs while burrowing his system of tunnels, and Ombric cast his mind about for bits of dark magic that might be creeping into the world. As for North, he was being rather secretive. He kept to himself (or, rather, to his elfin friends), working quietly and diligently in the great study, deep at the center of Big Root. On what he was working, no one knew for sure, but he seemed most intense.

And every night the children clamored for Mr. Qwerty, the glowworm who had transformed himself 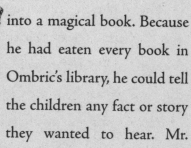 into a magical book. Because he had eaten every book in Ombric's library, he could tell the children any fact or story they wanted to hear. Mr.

Qwerty's pages were blank, at least until he began to read himself, and then the words and drawings would appear. But most nights the children wanted to hear one of Katherine's stories from Mr. Qwerty, for he allowed only her to write in him. But before any story was read, Katherine asked them about their dreams. Not one had had a single nightmare since the great battle.

There truly was *absolutely* no sign of Pitch. The sun seemed to shine brighter, every day seemed more beautiful, perfect, carefree. It was as if, when Pitch vanished, he took all the evil in the world with him.

Even so, the Guardians knew that wickedness of Pitch's magnitude did not surrender easily. They met together every day, never at an appointed time, but when it somehow seemed right. Their bond of friendship was so strong that it now connected them in heart and mind. Each could often sense what the others felt, and when it felt like the time to gather, they would just somehow *know*. They would drop what they were doing and go to Big Root, where, with cups of tea, they'd discuss any possible signs of Pitch's return.

On this particular day Nightlight hadn't far to travel. The night before, he'd stayed in Big Root's treetop all through the night, having searched every corner of the globe at dusk and found nothing alarming. Though he could fly forever, and never slept, his habit was to watch over Katherine and Kailash. More and more often the girl and her goose slept in their nestlike tree house, and so Nightlight would join them and guard them till morning.

Among the Guardians, his and Katherine's bond was the greatest. It hovered in a lovely realm that went past words and descriptions. The two never tired of the other's company and felt a pang of sadness when apart. But even that ache was somehow exquisite, for they knew that they would never be separated for long. Nightlight would never let that be so. Nor would Katherine. Time and time again they had managed a way to find each other, no matter how desperate the circumstances.

So Nightlight felt most perfectly at peace when watching over Katherine as she slept. Sleep was a mystery to him, and in some ways, so was dreaming. It worried him, in fact. Katherine was there but not entirely. Her mind traveled to Dreamlands where he could not follow.

In his childish way, he longed to go with her. And on this night, he had found a way to trespass into the unknown realm of her sleeping mind.

As he'd sat beside Katherine and her goose as they slept, he'd looked up to the Moon. His friend was full and bright. In these peaceful times the playful moonbeams came to him less often than before. There were no worries or urgent messages from the Man in the Moon, and so Nightlight could now enjoy the silent beauty of his benefactor. But a glint of something on Katherine's cheek had reflected the Moon's glow. Nightlight leaned in closely.

It was a tear. A tear? This confounded him. What was there in her dream that would make Katherine cry? He knew about the power of tears. It was from tears that his diamond dagger was forged. But those tears were from wakeful times. He had never touched a Dream Tear. But before he could think better of it, he reached down and gently plucked it up.

Dream Tears are very powerful, and when

Nightlight first tried to look into it, he was nearly knocked from the tree. He caught his balance and carefully looked at the small drop. Inside was Katherine's dream. And what he saw there seared his soul. For the first time in all his strange and dazzling life, Nightlight felt a deep, unsettling fear.

There, haunting her dreams, he had seen Pitch.

Nightlight and the Dream Tear

Nightlight Must Lie

Now, as Nightlight shimmered his way into the waiting room of Big Root, he was the last to arrive. He kept his distance, perching high on one of the bookcases. Ombric and Bunnymund were poring over a map of the lost city of Atlantis. Katherine spied Nightlight and could tell immediately that something was troubling him.

North began regaling Ombric with the news about his band of brigands and their new lives as elfin helpers.

Ombric's left eyebrow rose high; he was clearly

amused. "Well done, Nicholas. I see great things in store for your little men," he said.

Though neither man would say out loud how they felt, Katherine could tell Ombric was immensely proud of his apprentice, and North took great pleasure in Ombric's approval. She felt a surge of happiness for the both of them.

Bunnymund's ears twitched. *These humans and their emotions,* he thought. *They are so odd. They are more interested in feelings than chocolate!*

"Any sign of Pitch today?" he asked politely but pointedly.

North shook his head. "The old grump hasn't grumbled."

"None of the children have had bad dreams," reported Katherine.

Nightlight didn't respond. He knew otherwise.

Or, at least, he thought he did.

Bunnymund then answered his own question. "And nothing in my tunnels—nothing evil or unchocolatey or anti-egg anywhere."

Ombric stroked his beard. "Perhaps the children are correct," he mused, "and the battle at the Earth's core truly was Pitch's *last* battle."

North pondered. "Can that really be?"

Katherine turned to Nightlight. She generally knew what he was thinking, but today she couldn't read him. "Nightlight," she prompted, "have you seen anything?"

He shifted on his perch. His brow furrowed, but he shook his head.

It was the first time Nightlight had ever lied.

A Celebration, an Insect Symphony, and a Troublesome Feeling

It's now been eight months since we last saw Pitch. I think before we declare victory, it would be best to consult with the Man in the Moon," Ombric said. "And that means a journey to—"

"The Lunar Lamadary!" Bunnymund and North said together. The Lamadary sat on the highest peak of one of the highest Himalayan mountains, and it was there where North had first met both the Lunar Lamas and the Man in the Moon.

North was ready to leave that minute. It was a great chance to meet again with the Yeti warriors who defended the city. They had been quite help-ful when North had been learning the secrets of the magic sword the Man in the Moon had bestowed upon him. The sword was a relic from the Golden Age, and there were five of these relics in total. Bunnymund had one as well—the egg-shaped tip to his staff. The Man in the Moon had said that if all five were gathered together, they would create a force powerful enough to defeat Pitch forever. But peace seemed to be at hand. With any luck, the Guardians would have no need for more relics. But North *had* been wondering how he would keep his warrior skills sharp, or if he even should. With the Yetis, he'd again have able competitors with whom to practice his swordmanship.

Ombric turned to Bunnymund. He didn't even have to ask about making a tunnel, because next to making chocolate eggs, digging tunnels was the Pooka's favorite pastime.

"One tunnel coming up," Bunnymund said. "It'll be ready in twenty-seven half yolks—that's one day in your human time."

"Outstanding," Ombric said with a nod. "We'll take the whole village—everyone is welcome!" he added. "It'll be a grand adventure. We'll plan a celebration tomorrow evening to see us off!"

Katherine clapped her hands together in excitement. *Kailash will be so happy to see the other Great Snow Geese,* she thought. She'd wondered if her goose ever missed the flock of massive birds that nested in the Lunar Lamas' mountain peak.

But her excitement was tempered by her unease about Nightlight. She glanced at him, but he would not return her gaze. Instead, with his amazing speed, he shot out the window and into the clear, blue sky. But he did not seem bright, Katherine noted, and her unease grew.

The next day found Santoff Claussen full of preparations for the trip and for a celebratory dinner. The eggbots whipped up frothy confections, and the ants, centipedes, and beetles tidied Big Root while glowworms set up tables in the clearing—tables that would be heaped with delicious foods. Not to be left out, squirrels made teetering piles of nuts, birds filled their feeders with seed, and mouthwatering smells came from every nook and cranny of the village.

That evening the children led a parade of humans; elvish men; insects, birds; their great bear; the djinni; North's wonder horse, Petrov; and one very tall Pooka to the well-decorated clearing.

The Moon was so luminous that the villagers were sure they could see the Man in the Moon himself smiling down on them. The Lunar Moths glowed, and Ombric's many owls hooted softly. Soon the children were jumping onto the backs of the village reindeer and racing them across the evening sky while Katherine and Kailash flew alongside. Fireflies circled their heads, making halos of green-tinged light.

Down below, North's elves ate plate after plate of jam roly-poly, noodle pudding, and sweet potato schnitzel, topping off the meal with elderberry pie and Bunnymund's newest chocolates—a delectable blend of Aztec cacao and purple plum—all the while asking North to describe the meals prepared by the Yetis (accomplished chefs all) at the Lunar Lamadary. It seemed that being turned to stone and back again was a hungry business.

Even the crickets came out into the moonlight to play a sort of insect symphony to the delight of everyone.

Finally, when all the games had been played, the food eaten, and the songs sung, the village of Santoff Claussen settled down to sleep.

Up in her tree house, however, Katherine lay awake. Nightlight had been the only one who had not joined the party that night. And it bothered her. As did something else: Ever since the last battle, Katherine found that in quiet moments like this, her mind often drifted back to Pitch and his daughter—the little girl he had fathered and loved before he'd been consumed by evil. In the final moments of their battle, Katherine had shown Pitch a locket—a locket that held his daughter's picture. She could not stop thinking about the anguished look on Pitch's face, or her own longing to be loved as deeply as Pitch's daughter had been loved by her father.

Does that feeling only happen between parent and child, a father and a daughter? Katherine wondered. She had lost her own parents when she was just a baby. It was true that here in Santoff Claussen, many people loved her and cared for her. Ombric and North were like a father and a brother to her. But that wasn't the same as a *real* family, was it? She couldn't help wondering whether anyone would feel that same anguish she'd seen in Pitch's eyes if she were lost to them.

And there was Nightlight. She sensed his current melancholy

The locket

He's never had a parent, she thought, *and he had seemed happy enough.* But now something was wrong. She would find out what it was. She would make him happy once more. And then maybe she'd be happy too.

That thought brought comfort to the gray-eyed girl, and soon, like everyone else in the village, she was asleep.

But a strange wind blew through Santoff Claussen. It caused the limbs of Katherine's tree house to gently sway. If Katherine had awakened, she'd have felt uneasy, as though she were being watched by a force nearly as ancient as Pitch. Whose motives and deeds would change everything. If Katherine just opened her eyes, she'd have seen what was in store.

An Amazing Journey
to the Top of the World

THE NEXT MORNING THE whole village gathered at the entrance of Bunnymund's latest digging extravaganza: a tunnel that would take them to the Lunar Lamadary.

With great fanfare, Bunnymund swung open the tunnel's egg-shaped door and stepped into the first car of the extraordinary locomotive that would speed them on their way. Trains were still not yet invented (Bunnymund would secretly help the credited inventors some decades later), so the machine and its technology were still a source of considerable amazement for the people of Santoff Claussen. Like the tunnel he had created, Bunnymund's railway train was also egg-shaped, as was every knob, door, window, and light fixture. It was easy to tell he was quite proud of his creation.

Ombric, North, Katherine, and Kailash, along with North's elfin comrades, the children, and their parents, scrambled on board. Bunnymund was twisting and turning the myriad of egg-shaped controls.

The Spirit of the Forest waved her shimmering veils at them as Bunnymund started the engine.

"Aren't you coming?" Katherine called out, hanging from a window.

The Spirit of the Forest shook her head, the jewels in her hair casting a glistening, rainbowlike glow around her. "I'm a creature of the forest, and in the forest I will stay. Petrov, Bear, the eggbots, the djinni, and I will watch over the village while you are away." The gardens of flowers around her seemed to be nodding in agreement as the villagers waved good-bye with calls of "See you soon" and "We'll miss you."

As soon as the train began to move, Sascha turned to Katherine excitedly. "Tell us again about the Lunar Lamas!" she said.

"And the Yetis!" her brother Petter added.

But Katherine was distracted. Nightlight hadn't gotten on board. In fact, she hadn't seen him since yesterday afternoon. She looked out the window as the train began to descend into the tunnel. *Where is he?* Then, as the last car heaved downward, she glimpsed him swooping into a window at the back of the train. She felt instantly better.

"Please, will you tell us of the Yetis?" the smallest William begged, pulling on Katherine's shirtsleeve. She turned to him with a smile now that she knew Nightlight was at least on board. She searched through the pages of Mr. Qwerty until she came to the drawing she had made of the Grand High Lama. His round face seemed to beam at them. "The Lamas, remember, are holy men," Katherine told them, "even older than Ombric! They've devoted their whole lives to studying the Man in the Moon. They know all about Nightlight and how he used to protect the little Man in the Moon in the Golden Age before Pitch—"

Katherine cut herself off. She did *not* want to think about Pitch right now.

"The Lamas live in a palace . . . ," Sascha prompted.

"Not a palace, really. But a fantastic place called a Lamadary." Katherine turned the page, revealing the Lamas' home, glowing as if with moonlight. "There's nowhere else on Earth closer to the Moon than the Lunar Lamadary."

"Now tell us about the Yetis," Petter begged.

"The Yetis—oh, they are magnificent creatures . . . ," Katherine

The Grand High Lama

said, but her voice began to trail off. "They helped us defeat Pitch. . . ."

"I can't wait to see it all with my own eyes," Sascha said dreamily. "Especially the Man in the Moon."

"And mountains so high, we'll be above the clouds," Fog added.

The children began chattering among themselves about the adventures to come, not noticing that Katherine had grown quiet.

She rose from her seat. She felt uneasy again, and the children's company didn't suit her right now. She didn't really know where she wanted to be—with the children or with North and the other grown-ups. Even Kailash didn't comfort her. She was betwixt and between. She started toward the back of the train. The only company she desired right now was Nightlight's.

The Chicken or the Egg: A Puzzle

WHILE THE CHILDREN WERE anticipating their first trip to the Himalayas, Ombric and Bunnymund were in a deep debate about which came first, the chicken or the egg. Ombric believed it was the chicken. Bunnymund, not surprisingly, believed it was the egg. But the Pooka had to admit that he could not answer the question definitively.

"Eggs are the most perfect shape in the universe," he argued. "It's logical that the egg would come first and the chicken would follow."

"But where did the first egg come from, if the

chicken did not exist?" Ombric asked.

"Where did the chicken come from," Bunnymund pointed out, "if not from the egg?"

Privately, each one believed he had won the argument, but publicly, the wizard deferred to the Pooka. Bunnymund was the only creature alive who was both older and wiser than Ombric. In fact, when Ombric had been a young boy in Atlantis and had first experimented with his magic, it had been Bunnymund who had saved him from a most tragic end.

Ombric had learned so much since he'd become reacquainted with the Pooka. He felt almost like a student again. But perhaps, he thought, he had something to teach E. Aster.

"Have you ever met the Lunar Lamas?" Ombric asked, eager to fill him in on their strange ways.

"Yes and no," Bunnymund replied mysteriously.

"It *was* rather difficult getting that mountain in place before their ship crashed to Earth back, oh, before the beginning of *your* recorded time. So we have what you might call 'a history,' but does anyone *really* know anyone? I mean to say, I've met them, I've talked to them, I've read their minds and they've read mine, but do I know what they'll say or do next at any given moment or what underwear they wear on Tuesdays and why? Do I? Do I *really* know?"

Ombric blinked and tried to take in all that information. It was an answer of sorts. "Indeed," he said at last. "Um . . . yes . . . well . . . all right . . . That must be how they knew to point us in your direction when we sought the relic." He glanced up at the sumptuously bejeweled egg that adorned the top of Bunnymund's staff and raised an eyebrow. "They would tell us only—"

"That I was mysterious and preferred to remain unknown," Bunnymund finished for him, steering the train around a graceful, oval curve. "True. Absolutely true. Etched in stone, so to speak. At least until I made the curiously rewarding acquaintance of you and your fellows. Most unexpected. Utterly surprising. And, as you say, 'a hoot.'" Bunnymund had developed a genuine pleasure in using the new expressions he heard in the company of what he called "Earthlings."

Ombric smiled at the fellow. "I like you too, Bunnymund."

The rabbit's ears twitched. Such obvious statements of Earthling sentiments never failed to baffle him. Yet, while the Pooka would never admit it, Ombric could tell that he was beginning to actually enjoy the company of humans—in small doses, anyway.

As they neared the Himalayas, Katherine combed through car after car of chattering villagers and elves, looking for Nightlight. North's elves were busily working on what looked like a drawing or plans for something. They cheerfully covered their pages from her view. She decided not to pry, for she rather liked these funny little men. But more to the point, she was on a mission to find Nightlight.

Then, as it always happened, she suddenly knew that it was time for her to meet with the other Guardians, and she could sense that Nightlight was there with them. She followed this feeling as it led her to the train's front car, or as Bunnymund referred to it, the Eggomotive.

They were all there: North in the back by the door, Ombric and Bunnymund tinkering excitedly with the controls. And out the front window she could see Nightlight, sitting face forward in front of the engine's smokestack. He did not turn around though she knew he could feel her presence. His hair was blowing wildly as the train blasted ahead. The sound of the train was loud, but it was pleasing, like ten thousand whisks scrambling countless eggs. *Perhaps Nightlight misses all the excitement of battle,* Katherine thought, watching him lean forward into the air rushing past.

She wondered if North did as well. He was humming to himself, a faraway look on his face. Something was now different about the young wizard. He was still always ready to leap into action, still loved conjuring up new toys for the children. (Just that morning he'd brought the youngest William a funny sort of toy—a round biscuit-shaped piece of wood with a string attached to its middle. When jerked, it would go up and down almost magically. North called it a "yo-yo-ho.") And he still continued to tease Bunnymund, whom he insisted on calling "Bunny Man" no matter how many times the Pooka corrected him. Nevertheless, Katherine sensed a change, a change she couldn't quite put her finger on. In those moments when he thought no one was looking, North had become quieter, more contemplative.

And yet he didn't seem sad or melancholy or lonely like Nightlight did. His face was alive with excitement. *What is he up to?* she wondered, hoping that, when he was ready, he would tell her about it. If only she could be sure that Nightlight would be so forthcoming. *All this change is so unsettling. Peace is harder than I thought it would be.*

North, sensing her presence, grinned and brushed

a lock of hair from her forehead. "Ready to see the Man in the Moon again?"

Katherine gave him an impish smile, and nodded yes. She could feel the train beginning to climb upward. The engine strained to pull the egg-shaped cars and their festive cargo up toward the Himalayan mountain peak. They were nearly there.

In Which the Man in the Moon Greets the Guardians with a Fair Amount of Fanfare

THE GUARDIANS EXCHANGED LOOKS full of anticipation. Even Bunnymund, who considered anything nonchocolate or egg-related to be of little importance, looked forward to sharing the news that they believed Pitch had been vanquished.

For the last few minutes of the journey the train was traveling completely vertical—Katherine had to hang on to North or she'd slide out the door. Then the first car popped out of the tunnel into the clear, perfect light of the highest place on Earth. A new egg-shaped Eggomotive station was in place, and the train came to rest at the outskirts of the Lunar Lamadary.

The holy men now waited on the platform in their silver slippers and billowing silk-spun robes. They bowed deeply at the sight of Nightlight, who hopped lightly off the engine. Having once been the protector of the Man in the Moon, Nightlight always received their greatest reverence. Their Moon-like faces, normally inscrutable, resonated joy at his arrival. And this seemed to brighten Nightlight's mood as well. But he was still distant with Katherine.

Old William and his sons, along with all the other parents and children, gaped in wonder at the sight of the Lamas' headquarters and the cool, serene, creamy glow of its moonstone and opal mosaics. Sascha nearly tumbled out of the train's window in her effort to see the Lamadary's famous tower, which was also an airship. Even Mr. Qwerty, his pages fluttering, hurried toward the train's doors to get a closer look.

Gongs rang out. Bells—hundreds of them— chimed in the wind. Yaloo, the leader of the Yetis, stood with the Snow Geese at the edge of the platform, and blew a silver horn forged from ancient meteors, as the Snow Geese honked a warm "hello" at the sight of Kailash and Katherine.

As the welcoming reverberations quieted, Ombric stepped onto the platform. "Greetings, my good friends," he addressed the gathering. "We've come to speak to the Man in the Moon . . . and to report what we think is historic news."

The old man was clearly eager to see the Man in the Moon and share their findings, but there were the curiously slow habits of the Lamas to consider. They never did anything quickly and were usually very, very, very talkative. And yet, surprisingly, it seemed that the Lamas were just as eager to proceed. It was highly unusual for them to rush for any reason, but today they whisked everyone off the train and directly toward the Lamadary's courtyard.

The Yetis lined the outer edges of the courtyard as the Lamas led everyone else to the huge gong at its very center.

The children could barely contain their excitement. The Man in the Moon was about to be summoned!

The Grand High Lama glided forward. He smiled serenely, then, with almost shocking suddenness, he struck the great gong with his gilded scepter. The sound was sweet and strong. It grew and echoed throughout the temple, then throughout the mountains around them until it sounded as though the whole Earth was humming a gentle "hello" to the heavens.

The gong itself began to shimmer, shifting from a solid metal to a clear, glasslike substance. And as the children pointed in astonishment, the Moon began to appear in the milky light at the gong's center, swelling in size until a face emerged from the craters—the kindest, gentlest face anyone could imagine.

The Lamas bowed, as did the five Guardians and everyone else in the courtyard. As they stood up, Nightlight and the friendly moonbeam that lived in the diamond tip of his staff blinked a greeting. North raised his sword in salute and noticed that it had begun to glow. So did the egg on the tip of Bunnymund's staff. Katherine held her dagger aloft exactly as she had when she had vowed to battle Pitch so many months ago, and Ombric simply placed the palms of his hands together and lowered his head even farther in greeting.

"Tsar Lunar," he said in a reverent tone, "we've scoured the Earth for Pitch and found no trace of him. Can you tell us, has he truly been defeated?"

The image on the gong flickered and waned like moonlight on a cloudy night. The Man in the Moon's voice was so deep, it almost seemed like a heartbeat. "My valiant friends," he said. "Each night I send thousands of moonbeams down to Earth, and each night they return clear and untarnished by Pitch's dark ways." As he spoke, a wide smile spread across his face.

Cheers rung out throughout the Lamadary.

"It appears

the world is on the cusp of a new Golden Age," he continued, "a Golden Age on Earth. And it is you, my Guardians, who must guide its creation. It is a task of great daring imagination and thoughtful dreaming."

Everyone's eyes turned to Ombric, Katherine, Bunnymund, North, and Nightlight. One old, one young, one from another world, one who overcame a most disreputable beginning, and one a spirit of light. Such a group *could* bring about a Golden Age. But who would lead this historic endeavor?

To everyone's surprise, it was North who stepped forward. "I have a plan," he said.

He sheathed his sword and raised his other hand, opening his palm to reveal a small paper box covered with minute drawings and plans. Katherine recognized it. *It's what the elves were working on!*

"This was a gift, one that I now pass on," North began, stealing a glance at Katherine and then turning back to the Man in the Moon. "A dream for the new Golden Age."

The Future Unfolds

WITH THAT, NORTH CLOSED his eyes for a moment, recalling Ombric's first lesson: The power of magic lies in believing. He began to chant, "I believe, I believe."

Ombric, Katherine, and even Bunnymund joined him, quickly followed by the entire courtyard, and the box in North's hand unfolded into a vast origami wonder.

A magical city seemed to grow out of North's palm. Ombric's eyebrows raised. North was becoming something more powerful than a warrior *or* a wizard. Ombric could sense it.

North tipped his head toward Katherine, whose eyes were shining—this was the dream *she* had given him when all seemed lost during one of the first great battles with Pitch! A dream in which North was a powerful figure of mirth, mystery, and magic, who lived in a city surrounded by snow.

Katherine nodded back encouragingly, and so North started.

"I have a plan for building new centers of magic and learning," North explained. "One village like Santoff Claussen is not enough, and to expand it would be to change it. What we need instead are more places where all those with kind hearts and inquiring minds—inventors, scientists, artists, and visionaries—will be welcomed and encouraged. Where children will always be safe and protected and grow to become their finest selves."

The paper city hovered in the air just above North's palm. There was a great castlelike structure in its center, surrounded by workshops and cottages. A tiny Nicholas St. North could be seen striding through the village center, with his elves and Petrov, his horse, by his side. And a herd of mighty reindeer. The Yetis too were there.

North bowed his head and waited for the Man in the Moon's response. He'd thought he might feel anxious at this moment; instead, he felt peaceful—more peaceful than he could ever remember feeling. He had shared the truest dream of his heart.

The Man in the Moon gazed down at North. He didn't need to say anything. His luminous smile said all that needed saying.

TO BE CONTINUED . . .

THE GUARDIANS ARE CONFIDENT THAT peace is indeed at hand, that they have successfully vanquished Pitch. But can it be true? Or is Pitch even wilier than they give him credit for? Katherine, for one, is not worried—she's more concerned about her best friend, Nightlight. But when she climbs the Lunar Lamas' highest tower to see him, something happens that will change the course of all of their lives, and the Guardians find out that there is another magical being out there . . . one who Katherine desperately wants to meet. She might have to enlist Nightlight's help to accomplish this . . . but is he willing?

———◆———

Find out in the next installment of

TOOTHIANA
A Queen Takes Flight

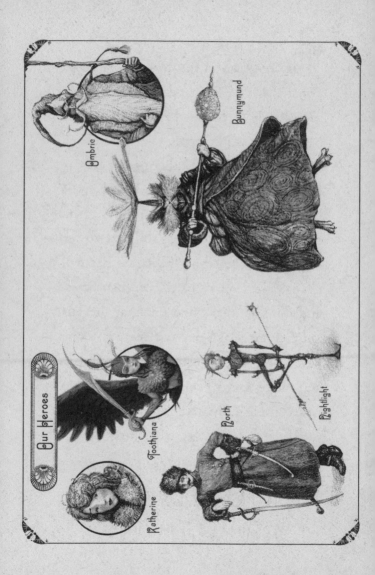

Our Heroes

Katherine

Toothiana

Nightlight

North

Ombric

Bunnymund

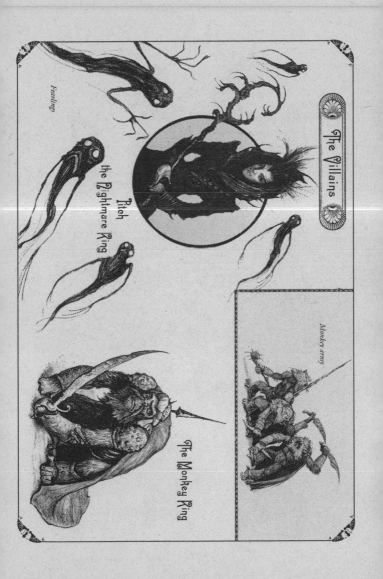

The Villains

Fearlings

Pitch
the Nightmare King

Monkey army

The Monkey King